Julie Armstrong is a walker and writer of experimental prose. *For Readers & Writers of Experimental Fiction* was published in 2014 by Bloomsbury. She has written for the *Guardian's Country Diary* and has a PhD in Creative Writing.

Julie regularly posts on her Facebook page: *Journal Of A Nature Lover:*

https://m.facebook.com/Julie.armstrong.3323

To Robert + Rachel

With love

from

Julie xx

Books by Julie Armstrong:

Mirror Cities
Dream Space

Experimental Fiction: An introduction for readers and writers.

The Magic of Wild Things
The Root and the Wing
Walking the Celtic Wheel

A WILD CALLING
Julie Armstrong

Copyright © Julie Armstrong 2023

The moral right of the author has been asserted.

Apart from any fair dealing for the purposes of research or private study, or criticism or review, as permitted under the Copyright, Designs and Patents Act 1988, this publication may only be reproduced, stored or transmitted, in any form or by any means, with the prior permission in writing of the publishers, or in the case of reprographic reproduction in accordance with the terms of licenses issued by the Copyright Licensing Agency. Enquiries concerning reproduction outside those terms should be sent to the publishers.

ISBN: 9798375204161

Cover design and illustration © David Colton

Moonflower Press

Typeset in Century 11pt by Moonflower Press, England.

For Dave, always

I find the notion of voluntary simplicity keeps me mindful of what is important: an ecology of mind and body and world in which everything is interconnected and every choice has far-reaching consequences. You don't get to control it all. But choosing simplicity whenever possible adds to life an element of freedom which so easily eludes us, and many opportunities to discover that less may actually, be more.

Henry David Thoreau.

Come forth into the light of things,

Let Nature be your teacher

William Wordsworth

One must have chaos in oneself to give birth to a dancing star.

Friedrich Nietzsche

Be the change you want to see

Mahatma Gandhi

The world reveals itself to those who travel on foot.

Werner Herzog on Bruce Chatwin

JACK

Did I kill you, Jack? What kind of question is that? But when they cut down trees, the gods of dis-ease crept out of the forest. There was no pill for your ill. Do you remember, I lost the plot? Transformed into a different character. Then shattered into a billion pieces. Was I told: 'I never want to see you again!' Or did I shout that at you, Bel too? I looked everywhere, but you were not there. I could not find you. And so, I was filled with despair. When you left, you took the sun, stars and moon. There was nothing left but doom and gloom. Yet, when I dream of you, I am a girl again. Light as the clouds and free, connecting with the wild side of me. Above the land, inside and outside things. Opening and closing my wings, flying so high in the sky. And as I fall, your leafy crown, sturdy and strong, catches me. I feel safe, savouring the branches of your embrace. Woodsmoke lingers in the twigs of your fingers. I feel peace and a sense of release. It is as if I have done nothing wrong, my folk song. I was lucky to find someone magical and kind, wise and true. So, why did I do that terrible thing to you?

Shame is a snake slithering in my stomach.

In my imagination I see you standing proud on the brow of a hill. Home, food and protection for so many, believe me, more than any other tree. Wild things curl in the curves of your boughs and nest in your hollows. A great spotted woodpecker

drums your trunk: tattooing, tapping, rapping
with his sharp, strong beak, licking with his
sticky, long tongue, among your nooks and
crannies. Insects and birds, shrews and beetles,
mice and lice, bats and bees, all eat and sleep,
shelter and breed, between your welcoming
leaves. But do not forget about me, beloved oak
tree. I need you, too, Jack. I love you. And I
love the bones of you, May, I think I hear you
say.

Ivy tickles my face, along with the lace of your
cells. Buds twirl and unfurl. As I lie on a
mattress of leaf mould covering myself with a
blanket of litter.   Your branches quiver. Then I
place my head on a green, velvet pillow of moss.
You toss symbols of good luck in the air, where

there are scarves of starlings flying in hues of
purples and blues. I rest my feet in a feathery
nest. And all the while a sigh reverberates in
your wooden chest. There is a wheeze and a
sneeze the rattle of dry leaves as you stretch and
sway. A jay lands in your twiggy hair. How your
nostrils flare when you test the air: woodland
duff. Puff balls explode in showers of brown
dust. I must ask you, Jack: Are you really
hundreds of years old? And is it true all trees
were like you in the beginning? I believe they
were, May. But how can that be? You are
unique to me. Oh, Jack, you are the fertility of
spring, abundance of harvest, spirit of the
wildwood, of bud, earth, sky and all of nature.

Sap seeps from the pattern of sun-burnt images

on your weather-worn skin. A brilliant lime ooze
on my hands, feet and chin. A frill of fungi
across my lips. Your faery door is close to my
hips. I taste the tannin of you. Touch the ley
lines networking your hands. Hear you speaking
in commands of light and dark. A stark moment
as I stare as your seeds scatter everywhere. I
trace each ring. My king of the forest. And I
hear you sing and photosynthesize. In a wise
voice, strong as roots, delicate as shoots, green as
chlorophyll.

At night I hear a little owl whoop-hoot. As the
moon silvers and polishes your bones. The wind
moans. Shaking you in huge hands, lifting
tendrils of vine, time after time, long fingernails
poking slime and slugs and snails. While

squirrels' tails curl around my neck. And oxygen fills my lungs. Bats dip and dive touching the mistletoe entwined in lichen. As I stroke your bark in the dark with utmost care. And doze. Whispering sweet nothings in your woodworm ears. Until spears of light pierce your canopy. And I am fully awake. But you are not there. Once again, I am filled with despair. You have passed. I have stayed. It is the worst of ways to begin new days. Without you.

My belly aches. Why did you forsake me, Jack? But of course, I know. And so, I rub my hands through my sweat-wet hair, gasp for air, riding the crest of a wave of distress. There is a pain in my chest and breast. If only I could rewind. Take it all back, Jack. What was I thinking?

The axe in my hand had a life of its own. You spun round and round crashing to the ground, bark splitting and peeling, leaves falling from your beard and hair, acorns tumbling from your ears and mouth and nose. There was the caw of a murder of crows. At least I think that's what happened. As I have heard that not all we remember is true. As Mother once said: 'Things are not always what they seem.'

Was it all a bad dream? But Bel was nowhere to be seen. She had disappeared like you. Oh, Jack, I am so blue. Are you too? Grief has stepped into my heart, tearing me apart, tying knots in my throat. You see, in my mind, I am still at the scene of trauma. Can you hear? I live in fear. I am your wife, whatever our past strife.

To think of that terrifying time cuts me like a knife. You are my life. I loved you then, still do, always have, always will, honestly, it is true, Bel too. Is she with you? Hope she is. Hear this:
I miss you
I miss you
I miss you.

When I fell for you, Jack, it was an exchange of visions. As you know, as well as me, reverie comes into its own when we live naturally. And we did, didn't we? How I long for those precious times. I was so happy living in our small, stone cottage. Our days had the quality of a faery tale. We grew our own food in the wild garden. There was Back Field, Green Valley, Seven Stars Hills and the river-that-runs-both-ways. And we lived such a connected life, away from the city's strife, in harmony with all the wildlife. But then on the longest day and shortest night of the fourth year, things started to go wrong. And I was not strong. Or am I imagining these things?

Now I am trapped. This much I know is true. What can I do? Speak to me Jack! I want you back. Where are you? If I ever get out of this hell hole, I will do my best to find you, Bel too. Let me tell you what happened to me, when you disappeared, my veteran oak tree...

TIME FOR CHANGE

There was a flood, a surging sea of mud. And for a moment the planet stopped turning. Yet, on the seventh day, I heard Mother say:

'May, the rain is going to stop.'

And it did. Abruptly. The sun came out. Mist rose from the ground. The water dried up. And I scratched in the soil what the voices of the land had told me:

It is time for a new beginning, a new way of thinking, a new way of living. It is time for change.

I did not know what the change was going to be, Jack. So, I followed the swallows, thinking they would lead me to you, Bel too, and we would

work it out together. But that never happened.
The sky darkened and the wind picked up again.
There was a deep rumbling and a grumbling,
growing and expanding. The land cracking.
Everything was out of balance. I found myself
running and stumbling. The wind chasing after
me. Getting nearer. Energy rising from the
earth, up through the soles of my feet. There
was such intense heat.   And a wailing, a horrific
keening. Was it coming from me, the screaming?
You see, Jack, there was nowhere to run. And
nowhere to hide. I was water in my own hands,
trickling through my fingers.

A long, low boom rocked the planet.

The Earth swallowed me whole, like a gannet.

And I tumbled down a gap, without a map. I fell
flat on my back, onto something soft and cold.
And I realized in an instant that all the things I
had always taken for granted were a privilege:
the ground I stood on, the clean air I breathed,
the fresh water I drank. It was rank. And scary.
Overwhelming. Life as I knew it was derailing.
And deep inside I was wailing. Raw, vulnerable,
fragile, broken. Roaming the wild places of my
mind. What did I find? Chaos. The world had
completely unravelled.

This is what happened, Jack. And I do not know
why or when this purgatory is going to end. I am
suspended outside time, inside a strange space,
in a tomb, the Earth's womb, frozen in winter.

THE PAUSE

And I am still here. For how long? I do not know. Preserved in snow. And ice. Spreading through my chest. Terror piercing me to the core. And I cry out:
'Jack! Where are you?'
But then Mother's voice in my ear:
'May, I am here.'
'Help me!'
'Be strong, it is wrong to submit to fear.'
'I want to get out of this awful place!'
'Discover patience. Learn from Nature. A planted seed grows slowly in the dark.'
'Yes, Mother, that is true, but what can I do?'
'Be firm with yourself and learn from what is occurring.'

'I will try.'

'To unravel is to reveal what has been hidden.'

Hearing Mother's advice, I feel myself slide deeper into the snow and ice, into the sound of silence. And there is such a stunned silence, Jack. I have never heard anything like it.

There is not a splinter of light. It is always night. It does not matter if my eyes are open or closed. It is as if I am wearing a blindfold. My mind is a blank page. I have been here an age. Still, I set an intention to submit to Mother Earth, until it is time for rebirth.

And as my belly expands and contracts with each breath, I make myself feel safe in this small space. Remembering what you once said, to me,

Jack:

'Space contains all things.'

I wasn't sure what you meant. And with my head resting on the crinkling leaves of your crown, I said with a frown:

'What do you mean?'

'There are infinite possibilities.'

The wind whistled through the branches over your eyes as you looked to the skies:

'You embody space, earth, fire, air and water too. This is something you ought to respect, May. Do not forget or neglect to give thanks for these blessings.'

So, I know there are gifts to be found in the ground if I hold the space with grace. And go with the flow of the universe, drift with the

current, beyond thought. And be with what is.
It is true. You knew, didn't you? What was it
you said, Jack?

'Learn to live with yourself in each moment.
Stop clinging to habits of the past. Nothing lasts.
Wait until the mud of your mind becomes clear,
and then, my dear, the right action will rise to
the surface.'

Yes, I remember that is what you said, we were
in Back Field, but was that before the magpie
attack or after? Whatever, it was a disaster.

I imagine the whole world, like me, is resting in
ice and snow. You too, Jack, I do not know, but
truly, my love, I hope so. You see, a long time
ago, you rekindled what Mother had shown me:
enchantment. So, I saw beauty, wonder and

magic everywhere, in the glare of the moon. The whisper of the roots to the leaves of the trees. The feel of the river and rain. The hugs of the wind and passion of the storm. The rays of the sun. Mother spoke in the flexing of swans' wings:

'Connecting with Nature teaches us all kinds of things. Remember, life is magnificent but fleeting, do not waste, embrace it.'

And meeting you, Jack, reawakened all that she taught me. And I was returned to myself. For a while.

Fear tiptoes into my head. But I choke it: dead. Breathing deeply again, pledging for the rest of my days, I will try to do no-harm to any being. I will live a life of meaning and dreaming.

Moment by moment. Engaging with experiences as they arise. As Mother once said:
'Life is a series of moments. It is wise to distinguish an event from your response to it every day, May.'

I do not know how long it has been. And I have seen. Nothing. Time has been erased. I am amazed. Have I been here for days or years? I keep asking myself: What is the reason for this falling: A warning? A calling? A healing? A dreaming? A scheming? A tearing down of the false to make way for the new, the true? A teaching for me and for you? And then I recall, what I had scratched in the soil...

It is time for change

And so, I learn to just be and not do, settling into the silence I am learning to listen to.

THE THAW

I turn inwards, lie quietly in my coffin of ice and snow, going with the flow of my breath. So, there is a space inside myself, fleeting snatches, separate from my thoughts. I break from my mind. And find these moments expand, become deeper. I hold uncertainty like an infant in my arms, swaddled with charms. And am present. Always intuitively aware that the world of the imagination is more real than reality.

I grow a wild wood. Winding through green tunnels, I find peace in the shelter of trees. They are my sanctuary, it is where I met you, way back, do you remember, Jack? Merging with the mulch and brambles and bracken. I become the patch I am walking on. Listening to the birds singing:

'This is history. Accept this time and learn from its mystery.'

Surrendering, receiving, believing, dreaming you into being. Your aroma is the taste of wood: sweet as wine, damp as fungi. And as I climb the oak tree, I find myself rubbing my face against dark-bark, treasuring you in my heart. Oh, how I wish you were here with me; maybe you are? What was it the song thrush once sang to me?

'Once you choose hope, anything is possible.'

So, once again I choose hope over fear. As I hear you say:

'That is the best way forward, my dear.'

I think of what Mother told me. The grain, the seed, drops back into the earth, waiting for rebirth, hidden through the winter, re-appearing as new growth in spring. And I hear her sing like a bird on the wing:

'Stay with the long dark. It will take as long as it takes. Your transformation is the Earth's transformation too and all who live there with you. This is a space between stories. The old stories are not working and it is nearing the time when a new one will begin. And when you wake, you will see with a different sight, a new light. Nothing stays the same forever. Think of the seasons. There are reasons why the snow melts, buds become leaves, change colour and fall from the trees.'

During this dark time of the soul, I hope I will

grow into a wise woman.

I feel centred, connected to the cycle of the seasons passing through my body. As. At last. A ray of winter sun pierces a crack. The light is coming back, Jack, triumphing over darkness and despair, bringing hope and repair.

The future arrives.

And there is a plunk-plink. I blink-blink. Drip-drip.

And my sense of self dissolves. Disintegrating, imploding, exploding, spangling, sparkling. I am the land, the sky, the stars, a billion years old fizzing into life. Drifting. Shifting. As Jupiter and Saturn align on the longest night, the shortest day of the year.

There is light and water, so life wins. And I am cleansed from sins. It is as if I am waking from a long, deep sleep, reborn.

What is this? A flame flickering towards me? Closer and closer. Burning more of the snow and ice away. I thaw.

And I see her.

MOTHER

She is standing before me in a glowing light. Woman of the wild woods and peat bogs, moors and hills, who prefers the company of flora and fauna to humans. On the palm of her hand a tiny-winged creature breathing flames of alchemy. And I burn to the very bones of me.

The woman is as tall as the mountain, deep as the river, ageless as starlight. Silver hair rushes down her back. Copper rings on her fingers and toes, one through her nose, bracelets on her arms. Her flowing robes dyed with the plants growing in the forest. Can it be you? Deep inside, I know that it is true. You will always be part of me and I of you. We are each other's flesh and feathers. She lifts her hand and the dragon flies free, circling me, before disappearing in a puff of smoke. Then Mother says:

'I am here to balance light and dark, life and death. And to help humankind face change and mortality.'

An arrow of fear passes through me:

'Is it my time?'

She shakes her head. 'No, May, you are ready to re-enter the world, not leave it. You have living to do, but remember death, like birth, is a part of life too. Practice non-attachment because everything is impermanent. You cannot escape death, and if you resist, suffering will ensue.'

I think of you then, Jack, do you recall telling me in the opening and closing of buds, you represented death and rebirth and I was your

Queen of Spring? You gave me a ring of wild flowers picked by your hand from the bountiful land and said:

'We cannot exist without each other.'

Suddenly Mother smiles and I say:

'Will you tell me a story like back in the day?'

'You remember the stories, May?'

'I remember how I felt when you told them to me. There was always a tingle down my spine. You spoke in rhyme. Stories old as time, steeped in magic, rooted in the landscape that birthed them.'

'No, May. It is time to create new stories from the threads of the old, to be bold and listen to the land speaking in Her mothering voice to the something evergreen in all human beings.'

'But who will be the ones who hear the voices

and share what they say with others?'

'We all have choices, May.'

'You are being enigmatic, Mother.'

And she replies with a smile in her forget-me-not-blue eyes:

'Am I ever any other way?'

From her robes Mother takes a large purse stitched with white feathers:

'Let me hand these gifts over to you. Open the purse with care. Inside, there is a wild rose to wear in your hair. And an amethyst, a talisman, to open your heart and assist in passing through the veil that separates the visible and the invisible worlds. A white candle to light your journey. Sage and rosemary to purify your way. White ribbons to tie to trees so your hopes and

dreams flutter in the breeze and never go away.
And a golden sickle to cut down mistletoe.'
Tucking the purse in the wide, scarlet sash around my waist and fastening the wild rose in my tangled red hair, I say:
'Thank you.'
'It is my pleasure, May,' she replies, placing a blue-glass, eye-shaped amulet on a silver chain around my neck. It is then that she notices me staring at golden threads woven through her swan's wing of white feathers:
'The threads are waiting to be picked up by us all. After the great fall it is time to restore, mend and lend a helping hand to each other.'
'To rebuild the world anew?'
'True. And do you remember all I told you since you were knee-high?'

'Mostly, but memories drift all around me then fade like mist.'

'Just as the trees drop their leaves, let the past go, and move into this meaningful future.' She pulls her long, black woollen coat tightly around her, stamps her muddy boots. 'Listen carefully to me.'

'Yes, Mother.'

'Everything in Nature has a gift for us to learn from. If only we slow down, watch and listen. Let Her be our teacher. The sky above, the Earth below, the moon, stars, plants, insects, creatures and trees all have their wisdom to impart. And all the elements reside within us.'

I tell Mother about the wild wood I grew:
'Through the long, dark hours the green paths

remained, keeping me sane, offering beauty, abundance, security, communion and companionship,' I say.

'I am happy that you are remembering what I taught you. 'And don't forget, May, it will soon be the cross-quarter day. Change is on its way.'

CREATION

We stand on a plateau and look up through the gap. My head spins:

'I feel disorientated, Mother.'

'That is no surprise. The pause was a profound shock which rocked the whole planet. We will have to go looking for ourselves again.'

She strokes my hair and at that moment, Jack, I haven't a care. The knot in my belly slackens. She asks:

'Do you recall when we sat with the trees?'

And I remember our time in the forest, a powerful place, where we took off our hand-knitted socks and rested on rocks. Smelling nothing but green. The robin whistling to Mother and she to him.

'Yes, I do,' I say. 'Our heartbeats were slow, letting us know that contentment was ours too, same as the wild things.'

'It is important to discover pleasure and appreciation every day of your life, May.'

'Like a blue sky.'

'And a butterfly. Rejoice in the fragrance of a flower, the dawn hour, the sound of wind in the trees blowing through the leaves, the taste of wild honey.'

'I will count my blessings and give thanks,' I say.

She lifts my chin, staring within, right into my soul:

'Pick up your thread and offer a contribution to the world. Something that is utterly absorbing to you. So, you can develop, grow, show and share with all beings to enrich their lives and yours. A gift you know, no matter how small, will make a difference.'

And then, Jack, without saying anymore, she rises. A bright star. And I follow.

Whirling and twirling we dance a new world into existence. There is the crash of boulders as mountains and forests fall from our shoulders. Water trickles from our arms. Oceans encircle our wrists. Soil sifts through our fingers. Creatures and plants and flowers fall from our heads.

There are landscapes of hills and plains, rivers and forests, deserts and mountains, marshes and caves. And then, as if coming from nowhere and everywhere, a spirit-like choir of sopranos sing:

'It is time to break the ecocide spell. Listen to the stories the voices of the land will tell. This is an opportunity for you to create the world anew.'

All goes silent

It is time

I have the swallow-in-the-air feeling I am waking and dreaming as I take a

L O N G L E A P

of faith

all

senses attuned to ways

once lost to be found

There is a sense

of

falling out of myself

into an

Otherworld

and

I land

on a patch of ground

stumbling and falling

hearing myself calling:

'I am reborn! And wherever you are, Jack, Bel too, I am coming to find you.'

JOURNAL

I am dressed in last year's bonfire and a tatty, white gown, covered in down and ribbons that have trailed through mud. I should bathe for hours as my scent is dead-flowers sour-milk honey-hum of wise-woman's castoff hobnail boots. I am alone with the rooks, grieving in need of healing, the planet too. There needs to be change, a new way of thinking, a new way of living, but what can I do? And then I remember Mother's words:
'Everything in Nature has a gift for us to learn from.'

There is the rasping of wings and I look up, thinking: creatures speak to us in so many ways.

A bevy of swans are migrating. Why am I waiting? A journey of one thousand miles begins with one step.

So, although underfoot is slick-slippery with snow, I connect with my energy and the power of the universe and go, keeping time with the land's beating heart and the language of the Earth. Treading over turf, marsh and moor, I follow the flow of life on a trail of hope.

And at the end of the trail, I discover a Bone Cave, a place for reimagining the world.

Inside, there is a strange stew of smoky smells. And something else too: fetid-dark, primordial. A taste of rock, iron. And blood? There are paintings on the walls of humans and non-humans. Ashy remains from fire pits are everywhere along with bat droppings and owl pellets. I rub a pellet between my fingers and thumb; it crumbles to greasy hairs, tiny skulls and ribs.

On the ground it is colder than stones and hard to lie on. Yet, I fall into a sleep, so deep, I do not stir, until morning is dawning.

Sitting up, rubbing my eyes, I am still so tired. And I think of the hedgehog who goes into hibernation for rejuvenation. So, I roll into a ball. Close my eyes, that is all I remember, until light waves scatter patterns of orange and pink and a blue hue. Believe me, Jack, it is true. It is as if the world has become as ethereal as a butterfly's wing. As there, standing before me, I see a pollen-speck of a girl, golden and tiny. She is overwhelmed, opening and closing her small star-shaped hands. I do not want to alarm her. So, I remain rooted to the spot, and say in a soft voice:

'I think we are cuttings from the same plant.'

She ignores me.

'You are me and I am you.'

'I've lost my Mammy.'

'Don't you know who I am?' I ask, but it is as if she does not hear. So, I say, 'you lose her to find her.'

She stares at me quizzically:

'You look like me, but my eyes are blue.'

'That's true, but everything is a trick of the light.'

She slips her small, star-shaped hand in mine,
and says:

'There are so many losses. I worry about the
birds and bees, leaves and trees and the plastic
in our seas.'

'And there are all the endangered species,' I add.
'Including me and you.'

'How true, we humans are in danger too. After
all, we are part of the intricate web of life.'

She sighs. 'And we are dependent upon a *living*
Earth.' And moving away, touching the
paintings on the walls of the cave I hear her say:
'Humans think they matter most but we didn't
weave the web.'

'That's true. I agree with you. We're only a
small thread and yet we think we are at the
centre.'

'Mammy would agree. She believed, whatever we do to the web, we do to you, and to me.'

I nod.

She moves towards me, taking my hand in hers again, gives my fingers a squeeze:

'I miss her.'

'I think she misses you too.'

'Mammy became unwell when they cut down the trees. She said it was a curse. Pa tried to nurse her back to health, but she said no one should take the lives of kin; it is a sin.'

'Trees are the lungs of the planet,' I say, batting the tears in my eyes away.

For a moment she is all silent stillness. Then she says:

'Mammy spoke of an era of greed. She said, Nature is not resources and profits. Yet, there are more buildings than trees and all the pollution makes us wheeze and sneeze.'

'This is true.'

'What a to-do. I wonder what will become of us?"

'I don't know, but I have been told Nature may have some answers, if only we know how to listen.'

She smiles and her face lights up like a lantern: 'So, let's listen to the chirping sparrows and watch the swooping bats.'

'Leaping dolphins and feral cats.'

'Stones and crows.' She screws up her nose and laughs. And I think, she says: 'Do you know where to find Pa?'

But I may have misheard her, Jack. So, I sit quietly with my hands in my lap as she has a nap.

There are moths bright-yellow brimstone and angle shades, greyish-green, buff-brown. And then bats appear: one two three four and more darting from dim, purple shadows, flapping in circles above my head, diving swooping. I listen to the bats singing. She wakes and yawns:

'Is it morning?'

'Not yet.'

'I am so tired.'

So, I pull her onto my knee, and she cuddles me: 'I love you, Mammy.' Honestly, I am sure she said that, Jack. Then she adds: 'We should live simply.'

'Absolutely. We must enjoy small things and stop thinking there's bigger and better and faster over there. I don't care for living in haste and creating waste, always talking of progress and profit. I have had enough of it!'

'We need to discover new ways of being. New ways of seeing.'

'Yes, we must pick up the threads of the old story and make it anew.'

'Did I tell you Mammy told stories too?'

'No, you didn't, but I believe you.'

'Do you?' She looks at me knowingly: 'I wonder how she will tell a new story?'

'Maybe right now, she is wondering how to do it?'

'I think she would weave together birds and bees, flowers and trees, create inter-species.'

'I think she will.'

'The healing is not about stealing from the land. It is about returning to an entwined, loving relationship with Mother Earth and serving all of life's beings.'

'That is a life of meaning.'

Together we smile and sit for a while. And after a year, or it may have been a day, who can say, time is an illusion anyway, I say:

'I've heard that one journey is all that's required to begin a fresh way. Come, tread gently with me.'

Then I wake up.

FIRE

I am cold. So, through concentration and much deliberation, I become the fire I long for, taking deep delight in the light, and feelings of safety and security. And it is as if you are here with me, Jack, coppicing and cutting out suckers. Placing dead wood onto me. And together we glow black, red and white for the rest of the night, slicing through the darkness. Rising from the ashes of ourselves, to be, all manner of things. Roaring and crackling, burning in arcs of sparks, leaping in flames.

And then by the light of the moon, a wolf appears at the mouth of the cave. She-wolf stares into my eyes. Howls into the sky reminding me that

I, like her, am wild and free, and must trust in
my divine feminine energy. I howl back in a
language to connect with the Earth and sever my
anguish. She ventures into my den, licks my
hand with her soft, moist tongue, again and
again, whines, yips and whimpers:
'There is a part of you that has wings and claws
and paws. Keep in touch with your wild side it is
there to guide you. Live in the here and now like
kin. Move with the rhythms of the seasons.'
Then as day breaks, she lopes away. And I hear
the ancestors' voices say:
'You have broken from the pack. Don't look back.
Feel beneath your right hand.'
I do, and find a journal stitched with white
feathers, a pencil: graphite and wood, which I
put into my purse. And the ancestors say:

'There is magic in writing as you know, May.
Write in it every day. Your journal is a safe
space, a place for reflection.'

'To write will be enriching and grounding,' I say.

Outside, the wind's icy fingers tug at my gown.
Snow lingers. Still, there is a deep knowing in
my bones. I am tuned into a different frequency,
treading in the footsteps of my ancestors,
walking the magic silvery trail, made by a snail,
hopeful that help will prevail, if I need it.

I pass bushes glistening with red berries and
stop as flocks of birds appear flapping their
feathery wings. Oh, how they sing. Watching
me as much as I watch them. Together we feast
until we eat enough, not too much; enough is

plenty. And as the birds' droppings scatter seeds, I pull up weeds around the bushes, for what I have received. Opening my purse, I take out my journal and pencil. Knowing in another life, I have done this before as I write in steady letters:

Giving and receiving is truly the natural law of abundance: reciprocity.

Day turns to night, and I light my white candle to show the path through the enchanted forest, a world of lucent green, such haunting beauty, holding healing energy. And as I thread my way through the tall trees, thousands of years old, I am told by their whispering leaves to breathe in unison with them. So, I do. And there is such a serenity that exudes from the trees and moss. I am not lost. A deep peace descends, starting to mend the wounds of the planet.

I smell damp earth and mulch. There is a breeze and the trickling of a nearby creek. Trudging over rocks that form the back of a sleeping dragon, I see, in front of me, the head and antlers of a stag or is it a Golden Tree? Whatever it may be, it is surrounded by five blackened trees: 'We symbolize the fragile yet precious nature of the forest,' they sing in high voices waving their arthritic branches. I write in my journal:
The trees teach me endurance.

And then I hear something or someone behind me. Adrenaline floods my body. Blood pulses through my veins. Whoever it is, they are coming after me.

SHAPESHIFTER

I hide behind a fir tree. And taking the amethyst out of my purse, nurse the smooth roundness in my hand. Feeling my heart opening I drop into my animal self into another world, sniffing and twitching. I graze with the deer and quench my thirst at the stream. Do I dream I hear them? Foot falls squelching through mulch. My senses are on full alert.

Who is this I am seeing half-hidden in the trees? An old man with long, white hair and beard. Is he to be feared? He wears a midnight-blue coat littered with stars, big shoes, a pointed hat on his head. He is carrying a staff and there is an owl on his shoulder. When I look again, there is nothing, no one. Am I dreaming things up again?

Moving stealthily, with my nose to the ground, hearing every sound, seeing with my hands, tasting with my skin. I look once more. It is him, right behind me, the old man I saw before but he is shapeshifting into something ancient and wild. And I recall what Mother once said to me when I was a child:
'Nature's world includes danger.'

In the shadows there is something solid, squat, stocky. Erect ears, short tail, huge snout, fierce tusks and there are bristling ridges along his back. Believe me, Jack, I am reeling. And he is squealing and grunting. There is a crushing of

pinecones. And a chomping of acorns and roots.
A snuffling. A snorting. I have wings on my feet.
But he is behind me. Galloping on stubby, black
legs. My ears are filled with the pounding of
hooves crashing though bracken.

My imagination sparks, ignites, I am on fire,
pelting to the wire of myself, travelling deeper
into the land, passing through the veil. There is
wind and hail, gust and gale, soil and sand, land
and words smelling of fur and feathers. I stop.
Panting and panting and panting.

I watch and wait.

My heart-beat settles to a gentle thud-thud.
Have I lost him?

But then the old man steps from behind a tree:
'Don't be scared of me. I was simply showing you I am the link between the natural world and the supernatural.'

My knees are weak, Jack. So, I nod, not wishing to speak. The owl flies from his shoulder onto the bough of a tree, listening as the old man steps forward and addresses me:

'Magic is all around you, woven into the fabric of the world.' He leans on his staff. 'I will cast a spell.'

'On me?'

'Yes, and another.'

'I will give you both the strength of giants for seven days and seven nights. Use your power wisely.' He taps the tree with his staff: 'I channel energy from Nature,' he says, staring into my eyes. And then to my surprise, he is gone. Yet, the acrid bite of after-fire hangs in the air. And I am aware that there has been a shift in my energy.

THE LADY OF THE LAKE

I crush rosemary and sage to purify my way as I move on, brimming with longing for a place of belonging. And it is as if I am pulled by a rope, towards a clearing, nearing a mirror-like lake guarded by a heron dressed in grey on this bitter cold day. Looking into the water, I hear my reflection say:

'Something is growing in your subconscious.'

And I feel it, Jack, deep as the lake, coming to the surface: a sentence. I catch it in the net of my conscious mind and I find myself writing:

What will the new story be? Meditate on this question until an answer appears.

Spirits rise from the lake swirls of mist. There is

the hiss of a swan in the reeds. I stand and stare as a woman, delicate as a faery, wearing a robe of samite, and a twist of gold round her hair, appears.

She rows a small boat towards me. Reaching the shore, she gives me a vivid smile. So sweet is the gleam in her eyes. At her feet, lying along the bottom of the boat, there is an edged, bladed weapon with a pointed tip that looks as if it is made from glass. She says in a tender voice:
'Would you like the sword, or would you prefer what I have in the folds of my gown?'
'I have no need of a sword,' I say. 'Can I have what is in the folds of your gown?'
Her brow creases into a frown, then she smiles and says:

'A good choice, May.'

And quick as a flash she pulls something from her gown, a fluid flick whoosh! I dash over to where it lands with a splash. And turn to ask her name wondering how she knows mine? But she is already disappearing back into the mist, lost in the dust of time. I do not mind, more curious to find what she has left behind. And taking a deep breath, I dive down into the murky depths to see what it can be.

HAG STONE

The silt sucks my fingers. As I pull something free. I am excited to see what it can be. The fleeting glint from fish scales as, like a secret, I rise to the surface towards a chink of blissful blue sky. Slowly I swim towards the shore. In my hand there is a small box, carved from oak wood, inlaid with mother-of-pearl. Head in a whirl, I twist and scratch, hiss and flap. My neck elongates as I open and flex my immense wings. I hear a mermaid sing as I lift into the sapphire blue sky flying over the lake and sea.

When I spy a strip of silver sand below me, I know that is where I will land. Tasting the tang of brine on the wind, I drop into the human me.

Hunkered down on a rock, I peer into pools of water. They are miniature worlds inhabited by periwinkles and sea horses, tiny fish and crabs, whelks and plankton, shells and pebbles, chunks of amber, green glass bottles and anemones waving their tentacles.

Far out at sea, I see a pod of orca whales. The grandmother trails with offspring while their mother dives for fish. And I wish my mother was here with me but it is not to be. There is the keen of herring gulls blowing across the sky like rags. The tide receding, leaving seaweed and shells and mermaids' purses. Oystercatchers dip their beaks in smooth, wet sand. A cormorant holds her wings out to dry as I wander along the tideline. There is driftwood, sculpted smooth, each piece carrying history. And I find a hag stone, a pebble with a hole; with one eye closed, I peer through it and watch a selkie slip out of her seal skin.

In the distance there are bright-yellow sea poppies, mauve beds of sea lavender and the crimson foliage of the burnet rose. Waves explode against white cliffs and sigh. Dolphins leap high into the sky like rainbows. I wait some more. Until I am sure, there must be a pattern and order to it all.

Dusk gathers in tones of purple-violet-blue. The sun falls from the sky: orange-yellow-red as the moon rises in grey-silver-white. And when it is night, I am bold and wade in up to my chin.

Then I swim. In a chime of colour: splashes of blue and green. The currents are warm then cool. I swim through jewels of star light. There is something familiar with the rhythm of the unfamiliar waves blossoming into foam flowers. I spend hours drifting. The sea cradling me in a huge palm, balm to my soul, as I let go into an expansion of consciousness. My cells are dying renewing imploding exploding surfing shrinking shattering disintegrating. Liberated and free in the sea. Nothing can stop me. I go with the flow, finding a way around all things, darting through shoals of fish, their scales winking and blinking like diamonds. And I am shrinking, sinking far below. Scuttling on the seabed, opening my crab claws, growing fins, knifing into a shark, then rounding into an octopus, waving eight arms,

then five, sporting spiny skin a starfish, back to
the human me.

The small box is still in my hand when I land on
the seashell sand. There is a deep hush no rush,
I lie there, falling into dreams of you, Jack.
When I wake, I give myself a shake and sit up.
There are five of them surrounding me.

STANDING STONES

The Standing Stones poke the epic, blue sky like giants' fingers.

Time stops.

I sit there awestruck and stare. Where did they come from? The Standing Stones are saying nothing.

Slowly a massive sun rises between them. And I greet a new world, that greets me back. The sky, lemon and gold now, pinking to rose, slashes of ochre, then a bronze-burnish glow. Shadows are deep-purple. The stones glow like garnets as the sun reaches its zenith, blazing fiercely. And only

then do I look away, hiding the small box i
sticky, salty hair, fastening it with care, next to
the wild rose Mother gave me.

As I turn back, I see something, Jack, lit by a sun
beam, and when I pick the rock up, it is as if I
have stepped into another dream, another life.
The Earth speaks to me:
'Sculpt the rock.'
And so, I do, until a woman's face appears.

That night I sleep in the centre of the stone circle
connecting with the Earth Mother, Banbha. For
the gift of her grounding, I choose holly berries
as an offering.

STONE HAG

Upon waking, I see Stone Hag riding across the land on the back of a wolf, leaping mountains to reach me. As she approaches, I see she has one eye, red teeth, blue skin and white hair frosted like snow. I do not know if the wolf recognises me. But she trots over and sniffs my hand, licks me with her soft tongue. As I run my fingers through her coarse hair to where there is warm wool. She grows a thicker coat in winter to keep out the cold. And I think like the wolf I must be bold and adapt as new things happen. She licks me again, then pulls away, leaving me with the Stone Hag.

Over her grey clothing, adorned with skulls,

Stone Hag wears a plaid shawl.   Round her neck a necklace of granite boulders. Over her broad shoulders, and strapped on her back, she carries a basket. In her left hand she holds a hammer which is, so she says:

'To form the mountains, crags, lochs and caves.'

In her right hand she brandishes a white rod. With a nod, she adds: 'I will maintain my icy grip...'

'But it is the cross-quarter day,' I say.

'What do you know, May?'

Yet, before my eyes, it is such a surprise, when the rock with a face comes alive. And without another word, Stone Hag throws her white rod to the ground, and turns to ashes.

BRIG

'Greetings, I am May.'

'And I am Brig, born from the ashes of winter.'

She is standing by a milky-white, bell-shaped flower wearing a cloak of the most glorious green I have ever seen. The curls of hair on her head are red like mine.

'Mother told me about you,' I say.

'So, you know I return every spring, when the birds sing, and the Earth is reborn?'

'I do.'

'I am a healer and a poet.' She pauses then says: 'Words soothe us, move us, transport us, to other worlds.'

'Yes, Mother told me that too.'

Her green eyes blaze with energy. It is as if she

is me in disguise. Only wise. She knows what I
am thinking because she says:

'You are made of me and I am made of you. We
are sisters of the one clay, May. But you are a
mother and I am a wild woman, a warrior.'

I do not like the sound of a warrior, Jack, but
Brig has this knack of knowing what I am
thinking. She says:

'Warriors are not what you might imagine.'

Bending her right knee, stretching out her arms:
'See how strong and powerful I can be. When I
take this pose, I know the nature of a warrior. I
can also be a tree, dancer, child, scorpion, cobra,
crow.'

'Yes, I know, but tell me some more about the
warrior,' I say.

'A warrior is not someone who fights, May.

Nobody has any right to take another life.'

I hang my head in shame, thinking: I am to blame for what happened to you, Jack.

'A warrior is a helper, a shield, a leader.'

'And now it is time for new leaders,' I say. 'Ones who will nurture, respect and protect. Every being has a right to be heard, all flora and fauna, no matter how big or small, we must give a voice to them all. We have had enough of greed, and those who seek power for its own sake, those on the make for themselves.'

'You speak with passion, May.'

'The old domination and hierarchies, conquest and control, broke the world. And now we are grieving for those we have lost.' At that moment, I am thinking of you, Jack, Bel too. 'We have to find meaning in what we have gone through.

Finding meaning is where healing lies.' I wipe the tears from my eyes.

'Don't cry. I can bring people back from the dark season into the light.'

'Is that your reason for coming?'

'I will take care of you and be true. We will reweave the world anew. Trauma and loss are something we cannot alter, but we must not falter. We can change how we live in the now.'

'How?'

'We can bring back the rain-makers, voices of the wells and those who cast spells. Magicians and witches.'

'Those who connect, create and communicate with Nature's force.'

'Of course. She takes my hand: 'Firstly, let me show you how we can dismantle the stones and transport them to where we can build a life without strife.'

Brig takes ore from the earth and before my eyes creates magic. Heating a long rod of iron until its tip glows. Then she strikes repeated blows, twisting and turning, earning my respect, forging tools to dismantle the stones and build a large casket.

'These Standing Stones are the markers of old bones,' she says.

'Our ancestors?'

'They are. And now we must travel far, dragging these memorials to the dead in the casket.'

And we do, Jack. We make the impossible possible. We have been gifted the strength of giants from the old man of the forest.

Following the sun, the permanent and eternal one, we toil, along stony tracks, bending our backs, round the sacred mountain learning to speak the rock's language. Creating movement between body and stone, working with ancient rhythms, of weather and rhyme, entering deep-time, trailing snail-slow into the valley below.

Later, when it begins to rain, we find a well, each of us focuses our energy and intention and chants a spell to help us on our journey.

We continue on our way. Passing bushes filled with spirits and sprites. There are red kites, buzzards and eagles. We discover poetry among

dead leaves. Bark peels from two yew trees
discarding words with smooth edges:
Kindness, compassion, belonging.
I place them between the pages of my journal.

We press on.

The undergrowth stirs with half-seen creatures.
We hear one say:
'Turn your cloak for folk are in old oaks.'
So, Brig turns her cloak inside out, a charm
against any mischief from the faeries. And we
lower our voices to a whisper, our hearts to
quietness. Our feet sinking into patches of mud,
still, we haul the casket behind us. Pausing only
to look up and meet the huge eyes of an owl
watching from the branch of an old oak. Do I see

you, Jack, a trace of your face? An acorn drops where I place my feet and not for the first time I am filled with wonder and amazement that someone as tall and strong as you can grow from a tiny oak nut. And I recall how you pruned your big branches at this time of year:

'To grow back stronger,' you said with good cheer. And the memories press down on my chest. The feel of your leaves in my hair. I am so aware of you at this moment, Jack. As we watch the aged trees shedding branches and leaves, preparing the way for seedlings and all other species.

Suddenly, Jenny Wren lands on my arm, she knows I mean her no-harm. In twirl of twitters, she tweets:

'It is not about me it is about we.'

And then she flies away.

We stop to rest for the night beneath the Graceful Lady Of The Woods.
'She is the first of the Ogham, the tree alphabet, and symbolises new beginnings,' says Brig.
And I think of you, Jack, the seventh of the tree alphabet. The tree of courage and the doorway to inner strength.

The next morning, as we are waking, we hear a moan and a groan. I sit up with a start, thrilled at the sight of a roe deer moving closer to us. And shifting around a trickle of fluid from her hindquarters and two hoofs dangle. Another contraction. And the fawn falls to the ground without a sound: new life. His mother licks him all over. And Brig and I slip silently away not wanting to disturb their bonding.

SONG OF CREATION

Guided by our instincts, we drag the casket over green hills and moorland, pastures and crags, marshes and steeply slanting slopes, rolling lowland, past water holes and ancient rocks, through sunshine and rain. One step at a time, singing in rhyme along with the enchanting voices of the land.

And I taste words in my ears and hear all the colours of sounds: roll vibrate tremor drum trill shiver hum murmur warble chirp wheeze chatter hiss boom rumble creak strum squeak. There is a cacophony of the Earth's history. A mysterious symphony of creatures and insects, trees and flowers, rocks and rivers. They each have their story to tell, about how we must treat them well, as they do us.

Over rough paths and hill tracks, we find our way, entering the mind of a crow, the heart of a flower, sitting with mountains and stones. We feel the song deep in our bones, body and feet as we dance to the beat-beat, in the heat of the spring sun and the cool of the moon. We travel on, knowing wherever we go, it is where we are meant to be, Nature will teach Brig and me. Walking the world into being, through a story full of meaning, dreaming a song of creation.

Brig calls: 'Come with me to swim in the river!' And I do. The water carving gently into the land, flowing and weaving, carrying sediment and sand. Silver rings rippling, reflecting, refracting light, awakening memories of you, Bel too, when we all swam in the river-that-runs-both-ways. Water slides over my skin, licking my hair. The water sparkles and glimmers with hope. And I am aware of the river teaching me to flow with the current, to let go, and move on.

Following the river's course, we see a salmon swimming upstream to spawn at the source, her birthplace. Leaping in the air, full of hope not despair, never stopping when the journey is difficult. And I learn from the salmon:
Perseverance and resilience.
And when I close the pages of my journal, I hear it. Bigger than a mountain louder than thunder, a deafening roar!

WATERFALL

Water falls from the high ground, tumbling,
rumbling, shattering into diamond-bright stars
of light. There are rocks and boulders marking a
path. They are mossy and damp and slippery,
but we scramble over them, clinging and singing.
When we reach the other side, I feel so alive.
Deer tracks lead us to a willow tree. Brig says to
me:
'There are still places that speak of wild things,
and all that has been, and all that is to come.
And we have found one.'
I nod, too choked to speak.

We rest under the tree, alongside the casket of
Standing Stones. Listening to the rushing river,

connecting with the land of our ancestors. And I tie the white ribbons on the branches:
'So, my hopes and dreams will flutter in the breeze and not drift away,' I say.
'A wonderful idea, May.'

We drink nettle tea, content as can be, watching shooting stars older than memory. Enjoying the silence, we fall into a deep sleep. In my dreams I reach out to you, Jack. I roll over and lie on my back, looking into the wide, clear sky shot with stars, thinking I hear your voice calling out to me:
'This is where you belong.'
'I know I do, but I wish you were here with me, Bel too.'
And when I wake, I see how the willow tree's

branches and twigs bend and shake in the wind, like the river teaching me to be flexible and move with life's flow, rather than resisting.

MEMORIES

The next morning, we resurrect the stones, feeling their language of bones, muscle and memory. I tell Brig about you, Jack, Bel too. And how Mother communes with creatures and trees, as she truly believes, they awaken deep knowledge of the natural world, passed down from the legacy of:

wise women,

healers,

witches.

Some villagers said Mother was a witch. They pushed her in a boggy ditch. Jealous of her wisdom and magical powers of healing, stealing her life.

But little did they know, Mother is skilled in the art of transfiguration.

I so often, think of our small, stone cottage, Jack. Do you think it will wonder why we are not there? Will it care? Or maybe we still live there as ghosts? I imagine the doors opening their arms wide, weaving their charms, sucking the outside, in, blurring the boundaries. There are poppies and cornflowers and honeysuckle growing from the sloping ceiling. Swallows and swifts wheeling through windows. Walls peeling back to a shell. Badgers living under the stairwell unaware of hedgehogs in cupboards. Squirrels in cooking pots. Frogs under the stone sink. Otters in the tin bath. Spiders in our old shoes, dormice in boots, bats in hats. Butterflies in cracks. Robins nesting in bowls. Crows in the chimney. Toads in our bed. A dog fox and a vixen in the shed. There was so much pleasure to be found in the simple beauty of the wild garden, wasn't there Jack?

I look back on our shared life with a bitter-sweet longing, a real sense of belonging. Recalling the moments of our lives preserved in the footfalls on the stone steps, fingerprints on the walls, marks on the wooden beams. Do you recall, our lives were full of dreams for the future, weren't they Jack? Tears well up in my eyes, I look up to the skies and blink them away, recalling what the river and willow tree taught me, to let go, flow with each day, not look back. And yet, Jack, I will carry the small, stone cottage's energy in my heart forever.

Do you remember when things started to go wrong? It was when the developers moved in. Trashing the land. Killing the creatures, plants and trees. Confusing the seasons. So, it was summer in winter and autumn in spring. And I waited to hear the birds sing, but they never did. And I became unwell, living through absolute hell, believing that the world was cursed. And yet the worst was still to come. You did your best to nurse me back to health. But then that awful thing happened. I cannot speak of it. It was my fault. And I am not sure what either of us did next. It was as if someone had cast a hex. But I do not wish for that dreadful deed of mine to darken our precious time when we cradled our hopes and visions. And so, I have a plan, my oak tree man. I wish you could see the seeds of ideas growing in me; I will nurture and coax them to become as beautiful as wild flowers. Then I will spend hours pressing each one between layers of land, preserving them for you, the whole world too. You see, Jack, one day, I will do what I am destined to do. And I hear you say:

'I believe in you, May.'

'Thank you, Jack, I am coming back to myself. But I am different too, has that ever happened to you?'

SNAKE

I blink my eyes because, to my surprise, I see something in the tall grass. I move closer.

There is a snake slipping sinuously beneath the beech trees. I feel a quiver of revulsion as he stares, forked tongue darting towards me. Yet, I remind myself he is kin and it is important to celebrate him. I hear the sound: hiss-bliss, as he rubs his flanks against stalks. Skin splitting. Sloughing off the entire length of him. Leaving it behind in the grass. Slithering away, new scales shining. Perfect timing, simply strengthening my resolve, offering his gift to me, a repetition of what I, and Mother had said:

The old ways do not serve us anymore. It is time

for a new beginning.

I write the words in my journal.

And I know that I have shed a skin and grown within. I am calmer, more mindful. We are all shapeshifting creatures, aren't we, Jack? You once told me that. And it is a fact that we are constantly in a process of renewal. Until we arrive at our true nature, the treasure buried deep within.

I have sloughed off my old skin. So, will you please, forgive me, and come back, Jack. I am sure, you agree, my beloved oak tree, there was a lack of understanding on both parts, but our hearts still belong to each other. Until the end of time, you will always be mine, as I am yours; I am the Green Woman. You are the Green Man. We cannot exist without each other; you told me that and it is true. I am finding each day harder to live without you.

SWANS

Over time Brig and I learn how to survive. We keep a bee hive and clear a small patch of land and lend a helping hand to each other to plant fruit trees, grow vegetables, grain. It is almost the same as how we lived, Jack. Brig whittles tools. So, we can we build a round house. And together we weave thin branches to make panels which we plaster with mud, which should, keep the draughts out, and the warmth in. The roof is thatched. And there are rushes and reeds on the floor. We fashion a door from rowan wood. Then Brig creates pots from metal, one is for lotions and potions, the other, for broth.

We like living in our round house, Jack. Every

day taking care of each other: sangha: from me to we. One day I fall and hurt my knee. So, Brig gathers ribwort and applies it. And the swelling goes down. Like Mother, her power is in the land. She forages for herbs, recites charms, casts spells. I scythe the waist-high grass while Brig tugs out the weeds. So, we can plant more trees. Digging deep in the moist ground enjoying the succulent sound of the suck of soil on the spade. Turning over the rich, earthy clods. Mixing in compost. Raking in hope. I crouch, watching worms tangle in pink threads of themselves. The hem of my mud-spattered gown sodden. But what do I care. I look up. And Brig is there, looking down on me, smiling happily. She hands me a pail of water to swill the soil from under my fingernails.

For days we watch the moon wax and wane waiting for the right time to scatter seeds, and when we do, we offer some to the birds too. When they have all been sown, we continue creating our shared home, by digging a pond for the frogs and newts and somewhere to drink and bathe for all the wild creatures.

Rather than talking about the creatures, plants and trees, I slow down and talk to them. Each day I say 'hello' and they say 'hello' back, Jack. A small gesture that carries so much love and affection. I mother them and they mother me with kindness and care. We are fair but firm, a friend and a guide, with arms open wide we nurture each other. A mutual respecting and protecting, so I am recovering a sense of stability and belonging, creating a gateway into the wild garden of myself.

Time is the cycle of seasons, of birth and death, the sowing and harvesting of crops, the keeping of livestock, making mead from hops. Working the land helps me re-find my place in the world. Slowly, I am putting myself together again cementing the cracks with buttercup gold before I am too old. Being in the groove of my life, having some sense of purpose and order, like it ought to have.

For hours, I make poetry of bushes and flowers, trees and leaves, pacing out rhythms and chanting verse. And in my journal, I write an explosion of words rewilding my imagination. It is meaningful and true. Still, I miss you, Jack. At night lying on my back looking into the sky I wonder why we lost each other. Sobs take over my body and I become a stream, a river, a waterfall, the sea. And when I fall asleep, I dream I am a sapling growing in the shade of my big oak tree. Buds opening, growing towards the bright-yellow-light.

One day in the wild garden I see a vixen. Her belly is slack from birthing kits. The sheen on her coat is of four summers. Her amber eyes meet mine. And I am aware that the connection is still there. She points her muzzle in the air, glancing haughtily over her shoulder as she passes by. I follow her gaze and see something lying on a boulder. Not two or three but four tiny swans on a silver chain. And pierced by a sharp dart of longing, I slip it over my head to lie next to my heart. Then, running my fingers through my hair, to feel if it is still there, the small box made of oak wood inlaid with mother-of-pearl; it is, so, in a whirl of excitement, I open it.

BRIGHT FIRE

Inside the small box I discover a name plate:
Bright Fire and beneath, there is a pollen-speck
of a rose, golden and tiny. My heart almost stops
beating.
'Can this be true? Have I *really* found you?'
And I recall Mother's words, when she said:
'Nothing is lost. Everything just changes form.'
And I say to Brig, 'can I introduce Bright Fire to
you.'
And she says, 'how do you do. I believe as a
flower you have a soul too.'

Our hands blend with the soil, sifting, crumbling,
a ceremonial act, together as one, we plant
Bright Fire. And watch as she takes root, raises

her face to the sunshine. Brig and I share feathers, put flowers in our hair, light candles, place offerings on the ground with care and whisper blessings. Bright Fire purses her rosebud mouth into a kiss:

'Oh, how I have missed my Mammy.'

Emptying my love into the earth, I say, 'and I you too.'

Adding nutrients of calm, gentleness, patience and peace, I release raindrops from my watering can all over her roots and shoots.

Over time I nourish and nurture our flower-daughter, Jack, giving her space to grow, weeding and feeding, watering and restoring with my green fingers, saying:

'Grow strong. Grow resilient. Live fully, love

wisely. Share and care for yourself and others.
Learn to listen to the little voice within. And
become the rose you wish to be.'

And her petals smile at me so sweetly. Gently I
touch one of her buds which unfolds into a honey
scented rose. And she grows and grows in love's
rich earth our flower-daughter, Jack. Springing
up, taller than me. Climbing over hawthorn
hedges, scrambling into trees, opening her glossy
green leaves, higher and higher, into the mauve
sky, filling the whole world with a light, so
bright, even at night, her blooms glow. You
would be so proud, Jack. Do you recall our
daughter was a seed sown in the wild wood? Me
rolling onto my back, then my side to see birds in
your eyes. A gentle slow-slide, you slip-stitched
into me, filling me with life, wife of the Green

Man.

Each day I see more butterflies on her stamens.
And there are bees in her ears, as I snip-snip
with my shears, dead-head her faded flowers.
Making room for new buds to bloom. And one
day she says:
'It's spring. I'm wearing my new frock, Mammy,'
lifting the frills of her lemon petticoat, arranging
golden petals on top. She gives a twirl as
ladybugs swirl from her tender new shoots.
There are caterpillars living on her too. And she
asks one to dance. And they prance, tripping to
the sound of the breeze playing with her briars,
scattering petals. Bumble bees join in, buzzing
to the beat in the heat of the sun, having so much
fun.

'They make me happy, Mammy,' she says. 'I provide a home for them and they take my nectar and pollinate me in return. I am learning this is the best way to be: reciprocity.'

'I agree.'

And she smiles with her stems at the butterflies and bumble bees, sharpening her thorns to the greenest of greens, puffing out her big bushy sleeves of leaves. Our flower-daughter blooms and blooms, Jack, as I knew she would if I nurtured her. And I do. Until the time has come for me to say:

'There is only so much I can do, Bright Fire, the rest is up to you now.'

'I know, Mammy.'

The wind brushes her fingers over Bright Fire's stamens. Speaking in scented whispers, making perfume with her petals:

'You have done your very best for me, Mammy, tuning into the temperature and wind, sun and pests: stripping black spot, not letting aphids breed colonies, pruning powdery mildew shoots, ensuring my roots grow deep in the ground. Paying full attention to me, Mammy, giving what you can so I have survived and thrived.'

'But I can't hurry the season of your growth, Bright Fire. I have given the most I can and I am sure you will give back to the world. Offering love and simple beauty, so there is less stress and more tenderness for everyone.'

Then I see him, Jack. There is a purple-blue hue to his wing and a green gloss to his tail. And I know he recognises my face. My heart starts to race when he lands on my head, but instead of pecking me, he flies off again, calling a warning.

Then catastrophe strikes.

RAIN DANCE

The clouds do not appear for days and days and Bright Fire wilts in the heat haze. There is the sound of crackling. And a sinister creeping of smoke. Brig and I see it getting nearer. Flames leaping and galloping all over the land burning down woods and fields. We fear for all of the fauna and flora and our lives too.

Brig and I fill buckets of water and rush to quench the flames. The sweat is running down my back, Jack. It is terrifying, and I am starting to become weak, but Brig shrieks:
'Keep going!'
Bright Fire cries, big tears falling from the tiny leaves of her eyes, pollen running down her

stalks:

'Mammy, I am longing for a drink.'

'I would be a liar if I told you we had water. I am so sorry, my flower-daughter, but there is not even a single cup. We have used it all up trying to put out the fire.'

Her buds droop. Her petals quiver:

'But my thorns are singed and my roots are scorched.'

She gives me an aching look. And I am yearning to help her, Jack, but what can I do?

'Have you a spell that can make me well, Mammy?'

Then she sighs to her roots and curls on the ground like a child sleeping. I peer into the cloudless blue sky and cry:

'Help me!'

Then without any warning, and not knowing why, I leap into the sky, dancing over the wild garden, Brig joining me.

The sky darkens. Clouds boil and burst. Rain falling in fat drops, spots pocking the earth, quenching its thirst. We cheer to welcome the rain. And there is the scent of wet soil and grass as the Earth offers Her thanks, as we do. And dripping wet, we lift our faces to the sky, and cry:

'Blessed be. We will never forget the value of water!'

Opening our mouths, drinking in great gulps, Bright Fire too. She grows so tall, stretching her green limbs, petals flushing red and gold. Thorns spiking, buds blooming. Her gorgeous fragrance brightening up the whole planet.

CYCLES OF THE SEASONS

In our round house, Brig, the hearth keeper, kindles the fire long into the night, feeding the flames with turf from out of the earth which carries the trees and fields. She hangs a cooking pot where it will boil, and sits cross-legged before it, adding vegetables and herbs. Pungent scents fill my senses. The room is lit by the glow of the moon and the flames of the fire.

We see a shape at the window.

And suddenly there is a knock at the door.

She bewitches me standing there. A woman wearing a hooded cloak. Her voice sounds as if it is from far away, an Otherworld:

'Can I come in?'

'Certainly, Mother. I am so happy to see you.'

As she steps inside, she pushes the hood from her head. And I see her swan's wing instead of an arm. Silver hair rushes down her back. And when I stare into her forget-me-not blue eyes, I see myself reflected there.

And Brig places a fresh log on the fire. There is the sound of crackling wood. I offer her a chair, but she squats on her haunches, wraps her cloak tightly under her chin, staring into the embers. Brig gives her a bowl of broth from the cooking pot and a crust of bread.

'Thank you for welcoming me,' she says in a language I have known since birth, one that sings of the Earth.

'I am pleased to meet you,' says Brig, snapping a twig in the hearth.

'And I you,' replies Mother. 'Merry meet. Many blessings too.'

She eats slowly. The wind rattles the door. And when she hands the empty bowl to me, I say:

'Would you like some more?'

She shakes her head. 'Thank you but I am replete.' And getting to her feet she asks: 'Are you ready for the next step, May?'

'I am fearful, Mother,' I say, 'but I know it is time.'

'Painful as it is, we must all let go of what we have been.'

'I agree,' says Brig. 'Everything grows old,

decays and dies. And yet, we must be aware that each season of life brings something special, something new, something we can learn from.' Mother smiles with her forget-me-not blue eyes: 'We must make friends with change, May, and acknowledge our age same as the rhythms and cycles of nature. Accept who, and where, we are in the dance of life. We are constantly changing, nothing lasts, this is the transitory nature of all life. Also, we are not a thing, but a becoming, a process of continuous transformation.'

Suddenly shadows of swans' wings flap over the walls of our home. And Mother leans her long, white neck backwards and sings. Bells ring. The air vibrates, boundaries blur. There is an opening in my mind. And I find I am one, and I am many: Bright Fire, Brig, May, Mother, all standing in a line of cut-out paper-people holding hands; and within each one I am to be found. I reintroduce myself to myself, in all the four seasons, the cycles which mirror the moon's phases and the elements. Who I was, who I am now, and who I might yet be-come...

And then a blackbird is singing. As the atmosphere changes, rearranges space, so something timeless, beyond form, becomes present, the energy of life: *chi.*

A NEW STORY

Opening my journal, I read:

To unravel is to reveal what has been hidden.

And as I process all the notes, I have written I reconnect with what I once knew before. I do not have to think about it anymore, it is time to unlock my door and share the ancient Earth's wisdom.

Realizing the essence of who I am and what I am here to do, I will explore my calling and offer what I can to the world. And in so doing, I will uncover meaning, find healing by reshaping and reimagining a new way of living.

My hand is itching, fingers twitching to start

creating a whole new story for our species. After all, stories, like the land, connect us and give us a sense of belonging.

Heart pitter-pattering with excitement again, I stitch together the threads of my learning: thoughts, observations and feelings, creating a narrative from all what Nature has taught me.

I write through December, January, February, March to the end of April.

During the pause I fell through the gap, without a map, but now I have one, a story to pass on to the next generation.

And now, after a rest, it is time to complete the

rest of my quest. I am coming to find you, Jack.

MISTLETOE

I smell spring on the wind's breath.

'Magic is possible today,' I recall hearing Mother say on the first of May. 'This is the time when the male and female energies join and bless the fertility of the land. But watch out for faeries who will try and entice you away.'

I wash my hands and face in the early morning dew and my dirty gown in a stream, all the time thinking of you, Jack. For hours I make a crown from the spring flowers. And when I am ready, I take it, steady-walking with the journal in my purse, with all I have written in verse. There is the scent of the hawthorn hedge loaded with milky-rose blossom.

Then I see the swallows flying high in the sky. And I follow.

Suddenly my heart almost explodes in my chest. Have I completed my quest? Can it really be you my sacred oak tree, who I see standing proud on the brow of a hill? And there is a bonfire too, nine sacred trees burning: white willow, alder, apple, ash, birch, cedar, hawthorn, rowan and oak. On the breeze a whiff of smoke.

'Jack! It is true; it is you!'

My wild man of the woods wearing your best jerkin of primroses and celandines, lady smock and cowslips, around your hips there are green ribbons. I stop. And stare. Completely unaware of anything else.

Arms open wide, my strides become bigger and BIGGER until I am running, so fast, at last, I am able to leap over the bonfire as you reach out your boughs for me. As I throw my arms round your girth, the world turns the colour of joy: 'You will always be mine. Until the end of time. I cannot exist on this Earth without you and you cannot exist without me.'

And I see your face peering out from a space between the glossy, verdant foliage of your hair, those sage-green eyes looking into mine. Time is a songbird singing so sweetly. I gaze down at the roots of your feet: grounded.

'You are the one who towers above all the other trees. You have seen so many wonderful things throughout your history,' I say.

'To fall in love is such a rare and fortuitous thing, May.'

'I am engraved in your rings. You give my heart wings.'

Acorns drop to my feet. Your smile makes me complete:

'Oh, you are the spirit of nature's rebirth. A symbol of fertility and mystery, rooted in history. You put fire in my belly, Jack, when you roll me onto my back. I will breathe life into you too.' And I do, offering hot lips, pink kisses. Then I stand back to watch you grow into your gorgeous coat of green. You are broader and taller than ever before, shimmering with buds, bursting with handfuls of leaves.

'This is not a dream, is it, Jack? It *really* is you gazing down on your queen?'

Shaking your leaves, wobbling your knees. You speak in spores, your jaws and whorls sounding like the chatter of corvids. Your consoling voice lifts over the rookeries:

'Sometimes things *are* what they seem.'

There are birds' nests in your beard. And I am aware your trunk is riddled with woodpecker holes. Voles and bees weave in and out of your fingers and toes. While wasps and hornets pour from your nose. And I listen to your orchestra of whistles rustles whispers and hoots as I step into the lee of you. Putting my hand on your bark, feeling your heart beating, beating, beating.
'My tree of life.'
'No more strife, my wife. We are home.'
'Let me stroke your glistening green skin.'
And I do. And you stroke me too.
'Oh, Jack, I am sheltered and safe, transcending time and space, experiencing oneness with you and Mother Earth.'

It is then that I place my open journal at the base of your trunk, drunk on happiness, offering my gift to Nature.

And caressing me with your branches, I become you, and you become me, we two, as one, fe-male energy: *chi.* Our roots dig-deep as we reach for the sky. And something magical begins. Peace descends. Our broken hearts mend.

Then I climb up your limbs, clasping gnarled, knotty fingers. The sap rising through your veins and up your trunk. Your boughs swing as I cling, hollows providing hand-holds, branches foot-holds. Pushing my face through leaves. As your canopy closes carefully around me in a gentle embrace, touching my arms, legs and face, my ancient man of the forest:

'You are so wise.'

Closing your eyes as I finally haul myself up to a fork in your branches. Jenny Wren darts out singing the longest, loudest most intricate song of your soul. And I am transported to some higher place. Sitting on your crown, I gaze down, staring at the exquisite landscape, joy rising in me, bursting like a seed, my head scattering gratitude and appreciation. Then I look up into a space above the treetops. Until Jack calls to me:

'Cut the ball of mistletoe left to grow by the sky gods!'

'But it is too early.'

'This is an auspicious day, May. I have the love of my life back.'

'I will do what you say, Jack.'

'And let it fall to the ground without a sound.'

So, I s-t-r-e-t-c-h and at last reach the mistletoe, evergreen leaves, white, waxy berries. Wobbling momentarily, yet your branches hold me, tongues of leaves whispering in my ear:

'I have you safe, my dear.'

My mind is still. A lamp in a windless place not flickering.

Clutching the sacred plant, I cut with the golden sickle and watch the ball fall away, fertilising the earth, giving birth to my story.

How The Teachings Of Nature & Yoga Can Bring About Meaningful Change For A Better Future

We have been telling disaster and climate-crisis stories for some time now. Doom and gloom narratives with visions of dystopian futures building on the urgencies of: global warming, climate- change, pollution, wild fires, flooding, species extinction, biodiversity and habitat loss. Indeed, I have written about these things myself. During the first lockdown, Spring 2020, I wrote, and published an essay, which became a springboard for my prose-poem: *The Magic Of Wild Things,* that bears witness to our times, highlighting ecological fears and giving voice to an oak tree felled by 'developers'. And so, as the *The Magic Of Wild Things*, concludes, May, my protagonist writes in the soil:

It is time for a new beginning, a new way of thinking, a new way of living. It is time for change.

After finishing the book, I knew this sentence was the beginning of another work which would be about the change, but what? I pondered this question for a long time, whilst out walking in the countryside, during my yoga and creative writing practices. I also turned to the poets and Nature to see what I could glean from them too. Their wisdom was bountiful. And so, drawing upon all of my spiritual practices, I have written a sequel to *The Magic Of Wild Things*, what I hope is a celebratory novella: *A Wild Calling*. It is my intention that his work shows how we can imagine, and ultimately bring about meaningful change, for all sentient beings. Indeed, it is important to note that by engaging in yoga: meditation, philosophical ideas, mudras, mantras, postures, breathing exercises, we 'yoke' ourselves to a spiritual discipline to bring about positive change. I suggest by walking in the natural world, and engaging with any creative work, also ensues change will ultimately take place.

A Wild Calling is not about power and greed, human supremacy and entitlement, rather, it shows human beings are no more important than any flora and fauna. We are all kin, or as the late Vietnamese Buddhist monk, Thich Nhat Hanh, said: we are 'interbeing'. As it is written in the *Upanishads*: 'Those who see all creatures within themselves and themselves in all creatures know no fear. Those who see all creatures in themselves and themselves in all creatures know no grief. How can the multiplicity of life delude the one who sees its unity?' *Upanishad 6-7*. The notion of the interconnectedness of things is a predominant theme in the novella. In Vedic narrative, the divine, natural world and human world are inseparable.

The Confucian scholar Fang Yizhi (1611-71) concluded that *qi* is an energy that pervades all life linking human, animal and plants. Chinese religious traditions believe in Yin and Yang, two opposing forces which exist within *qi*. These forces reside in all elements of the universe, including humans, and are engaged in a process of continual transformation. Indeed, we are all one body and we share the same energy. As Buddha said: 'We inter-breathe with the forests, we drink from oceans. They are part of our own body'. This is a view shared by the Romantic poet, Samuel Coleridge. In The *Eolian Harp* he refers to the 'one life' uniting the whole of reality; this same concept is the focus of his most famous poem *The Rime Of The Ancient Mariner* which speaks to our current environmental crisis too. The writer and graphic artists Nick Hayes created a graphic novel: *The Rime of The Modern Mariner* in 2011, a re-working of Coleridge's poem. Percy Shelley also writes of the unity of all things in *Love's Philosophy*: 'Nothing in the world is single:/All things by a law divine/ In one spirit meet and mingle'.

Each character in *A Wild Calling,* that is:
May, Mother, Jack, Brig and Bright Fire live connected, helping us reimagine the world and ourselves, inspiring new ideas so we grow, change and become guardians of the land, once more, same as our ancestors. The natural world, therefore, is not then simply a backdrop to their concerns, it *is* their concern, and is foregrounded in the work.

Barack Obama said, at the United Nations Climate Change Conference, 8th November, 2021:
'Our planet has been wounded by our actions. Those wounds won't be healed today or tomorrow

or the next. But they can be healed by degrees. If we start with that spirit, if each of us can fight through the occasional frustration and the dread, if we all do our part and follow through our commitment, I believe we can secure our future. We have to. And what a profound and noble task we have set for ourselves'.

The characters in *A Wild Calling* speak of, and encounter, the planet's wounds: climate change, species extinction, devastation of land and over consumption. Yet, they show through the way they live their lives, their actions and deeds, that solutions can be discovered which will 'secure our future' and heal the planet. They show gratitude and appreciation for their lives, each other and the natural world, displaying kindness and empathy for all beings. As opposed to being driven by power and self-gratification, the characters create lives of mindful simplicity. They do not seek to dominate other creatures or each other, rather they share, co-operate and collaborate instead. A focus of the novella is on the spiritual development of the characters. Their lifestyles and attitudes, then, reflect the ethics of yoga, principles originating from the ancient Indian philosophical text, *The Yoga Sutras Of Patanjali*, namely the *Yamas*, concerned with the attitude we have towards people and the world around us. And the *Niyamas,* how we relate in terms of self-discipline. The *Yamas* and *Niyamas* are a moral code, guidelines for an ethical way of living. That is, how we interact with ourselves, others, the environment and how we deal with personal and universal issues. So, by respecting these ethics, as they do, the characters are mindful of action and cultivate awareness.

The *Yamas* are: *Ahimsa*, non-violence, non-harming in thought, word or deed and compassion for all living things. *Satya*, truthfulness. *Asteya,* non-stealing. *Brahmacharya*, correct use of energy. *Aparigraha*, non-greed.

The *Niyamas* are: *Sauca,* cleanliness, to be pure. *Santosa*, contentment. *Tapas*, self-disciple. *Svadhyaya,* to continue learning, self-reflection and to develop awareness. *Isvarapranidhana*: contemplation of a higher power.

May, appreciates and celebrates, as Tantra does, shown in passages from the *Atharva-Veda* and *Rig-Veda*, the five elements: earth, water, space, fire and air. She is seen contemplating these elements at different occasions throughout the novella; in so doing, she discovers, in accordance with the revered Hindu text: *Bhagavad Gita,* that God can be found in all things. May also learns, in in the spirit of Vedantic philosophy, she cannot change events, she can only change her reaction to them and seek to learn from the error of her ways and those of other humans.

The book opens to utter destruction and complete devastation, the consequence of a flood which occurred at the end of *The Magic Of Wild Things*. Following this there is The Pause, when May falls through a gap in the Earth and is frozen, waiting for rebirth. It is during this time, when she is fearful, that she learns to focus on her breath, a nod to the *Upanishads,* which honour the power of the breath.   And by coming to understand the structures and functions of her body and mind, May, gains insights into the workings of the cosmos. And when she finally experiences rebirth, and embarks on a journey to find Jack, she also continues with a metaphorical yoga journey, one which seeks to cultivate self-realization, mindfulness and inner awareness, which enables her to discover how meaningful change in the world can be brought about.

Following my time spent in the natural world since a child, I have learned that Nature can show us how to live a meaningful, sustainable life, if only we care to slow down and pay full attention. As William Wordsworth wrote in *The Tables Turned*: 'Let nature be your teacher.' Emulating the *Chandogya Upanishad,* May, like Satyakama Jabala, a great teacher of his day, receives her spiritual instructions from trees, creatures, plants and the forces of Nature; they offer guidance on how she can live in harmony with herself and Nature. She accrues a receptive state of mind by 'quiet sitting' in the natural world and meditating to clear, still and stabilise her mind, which, in turn, leads to her grounding herself in the present moment -*atha*- a greater appreciation of the sacredness of all things and transformation.

During her physical and inner journey May has the opportunity to rediscover, and embrace, her path and the parts of herself she lost in *The Magic Of Wild Things*. She does this by being present and mindfully aware and capturing what she sees, hears and learns from the land, fauna and flora in the journal she has been gifted. Ultimately, these notes and insights she records, become the story May writes, the story you, the reader, have just read.

A Wild Calling is a 'hymn', not unlike the *Vedas*, in which I praise Mother Earth and all she offers us: food, air, earth, water, fire, companionship of creatures, beauty of wildflowers, shelter of trees and the medicinal properties of plants, stressing the importance of protecting and nurturing our planet in an act of gratitude and reciprocation. I celebrate a sense of place and nature's beauty, through poetic descriptions of the land, fauna and flora, inviting readers to experience a love for the mountains, the rivers, the forests, for we 'protect what we love', according to the late conservationist, Jacques Cousteau. The poet and environmentalist activist, Wendell Berry, has expressed the same sentiment.

This book is intended to be a space where I share the moments of calm, wonder, joy, peace, insight and harmony I experience when walking in the natural world and during yoga and writing practices, in the hope that readers may also experience these special moments.

Author of the *Yoga & Ecology* course, on which I studied via the *Hindu Centre Oxford*, Professor Chris Chapple, wrote to me in an email, March 2022:

'Literature has great capacity to communicate important information and to effect attitudinal change'.

It is a view I hold too. I also share Professor Kathleen Jamie's thoughts when she writes:

'It doesn't actually take much to be an eco-writer or eco poet. It begins when you pay attention to the world, and to language, and strive to bring the two together. This writing matters. And so, crucially, does our reading…If by reading you are encouraged or confirmed in your love of the natural world, if your interest is piqued, if you're inspired simply to put the book down and look outside, then our job is done…when we read and write, when we just listen and notice, we are not little cogs in the machine, but part of the remedy'. (*Antlers Of Water*, p. xvii)

What more can I say? Other than, I am reaching out to readers, wishing to touch their path and in some small way, be a catalyst for meaningful change.

Collective micro-acts relate to macro-acts and if everyone plays their part, no matter how big or small, the world can be protected, cherished, loved, repaired, and remade anew for all living things.

Notes on scriptures & texts

The word Hinduism refers to a way of life, drawing its spiritual beliefs and wisdom not from a single prophet or deity nor from a single holy book, but from thousands of years of collective wisdom passed on in the tradition of storytelling. *Veda* from the root 'vid' meaning *to know, wisdom, knowledge* is a collection of hymns, poems and chants known as the *Rg Veda, Yajur Veda, Atharva Veda and the Sama* Veda and constitute the beginning of Indian philosophy. They contain creation myths and venerate Nature's powers: the sun, moon and the elements of earth, water, ether, fire and air. Originally the *Veda* were passed orally from generation to generation. However, they were ultimately the earliest sacred texts to be written down; it is difficult to say exactly when, but around 1500 B.C. Shortly after the *Vedas* were written down the *Upanishads* were composed.

The *Upanishads*, which delved into the nature of the soul, the mystery of death and emphasised the oneness of the universe. They present stories and dialogues in which the teachings are imparted, *Upanishad* means 'at the feet of' for the scriptures were spoken to disciples sitting at the feet of their teachers. From the bedrock of the *Upanishads* emerges Buddhism and Jainism which take a different approach from Hinduism but share many of the beliefs and practices including Yoga. Yoga develops concurrently in all three traditions, intermixing with one another, containing contributions from all three traditions. The development of yoga is complex. However, *The Yoga Sutras* of Patanjali, has come, as the first sutra states, to present the authoritative teaching on yoga.

The great epics *Ramayana* and *Mahabharata*, including the famous *Bhagavad Gita* or *Song Of God* were written later between 400 -600 B.C. The *Bhagavad Gita* forms one episode in Indian's Great Epic, the *Mahabharata*, based on stories surrounding the battle between the soul and the senses. The *Bhagavad Gita* contains the absolute essential teachings of Indian philosophy through a conversation between Krishna and the Arjuna, on the eve of the great battle at Kurukshetra, in which Arjuna is destined to fight.

The *Bhagavad Gita* was one of the source texts the 'Father of Yoga', a sage in ancient India, Patanjali made use of when constructing *The Yoga Sutras*, 195 aphorisms frequently referred to as the foundational work on the ideology and the practice of Yoga, a philosophical system for stilling the mind. The *Yamas* and *Niyamas* originate from *The Yoga Sutras*.

Ogham is an ancient *Celtic alphabet* made up of twenty letters, simple shapes, straight and diagonal lines, carved into wood or stone. Each of the letters corresponds to the name of a tree or shrub: Birch, Rowan, Alder, Willow, Ash, Hawthorn, Oak, Holly, Hazel, Apple, Blackberry, Ivy, Broom, Blackthorn, Elder, Pine, Gorse, Heather, Aspen and Yew, illustrating the importance of trees to the Celts. They provided shelter, food, medicine and were believed to be sources of magic and power. Some trees, like the Oak, were considered sacred.

ACKNOWLEDGEMENTS

I wish to take this opportunity to offer gratitude and thanks to all my wonderful yoga tutors over many years of practice, in particular my long-standing tutor, Lesley Wittering, more recently, Kristyna Vopickova and Sophie Ng. Also, Daniel Simpson, with whom I studied *Philosophy Of Yoga*, and Professor Chris Chapple *Yoga & Ecology*, both esteemed tutors at the *Hindu Centre, Oxford*, organized by Lal Krishna, many thanks: Namaste. Thank you to Geoff Sutton who kindly offers welcome feedback on my work. And to Dr Jenny Newman, a source of great inspiration. Huge thanks to my family: Min, Carl, Callum and Emme who fill my life with hope and inspiration. Thank you and love to Mum, Kathleen Armstrong, who shared her passion of the natural world with me; you are always in my thoughts. I am ever grateful to Dr Meriel Lland, thank you for your unfailing enthusiasm, insight, knowledge, loyalty, a once in a life time friendship, and for the title of this book. Meriel is not only a wonderful editor, and a delight to work with, she is also an eco-writer, wildlife photographer, artist and film-poet who has 'a passion to protect and conserve wildlife and ecosystems.' Her website is: http://www.meriellland.co.uk.

I am blessed to always to have the support and encouragement of Dave Colton. Dave's vision, energy, imagination, generosity of spirit, kindness and intelligence never cease to amaze me. Huge thanks for the glorious cover of *A Wild Calling* and for all that you do to help bring my work to fruition. And finally, *The Magic Of Wild Things* is a nod to Wendell Berry's *The Peace Of Wild Things* and *A Wild Calling* is to Jack London's *The Call Of The Wild*. Thank you.

Printed in Great Britain
by Amazon